BRIAN WILDSMITH

The SEVEN RAVENS

OXFORD

UNIVERSITY PRESS

Once there was a man and his wife who had seven sons. They loved them very much but they longed for a daughter.

At last to their great joy a little girl was born whom they called Anna. But she was so weak and small that they were afraid she would die. They sent their sons to fetch water from the well, so they could baptize her.

Each of the boys wanted to draw the water and started to fight. In the struggle the jug fell and was smashed. They stood there, not knowing what to do, and none of them dared to go home.

When they did not return, their father grew impatient and said: 'Those boys must be playing one of their games and have forgotten about the water.'

Then he grew very angry and shouted: 'I wish those wicked boys were all turned into ravens!'

No sooner had he spoken than he heard a beating of wings in the air above and, looking up, he saw seven black ravens flying away.

Anna grew up as an only child. One day she heard some people talking about how her brothers had been turned into ravens. She went to her parents, who could not keep their secret any longer.

Anna was so sad that she decided to go and find her brothers
and set them free. She set out, taking a little ring from her
parents, a loaf of bread, a jug of water, and a little chair.
She walked on and on until she came to the end of the world.

Anna travelled further and
further until she came to the
sun. But it was too hot and
bright there, and she ran away
in case she was burned.

Then Anna
came to the
moon but it was too
cold and bad-tempered.
'Go away! Go away!' it said.
And all the signs of the zodiac
took no notice of her.

At last Anna came to the stars, who were friendly and kind to her.

The morning star rose, gave her a magic bone, and said: 'You will find your brothers inside the Glass Mountain. But you cannot open the Glass Mountain without this magic bone.'

Anna took the magic bone and wrapped it carefully in a piece of cloth.

She travelled on for many days until at last she reached the Glass Mountain.

The door into the Glass Mountain was shut. She opened the cloth to take out the bone, but the cloth was empty. She had lost the star's magic gift. What was she to do without a key? Quickly she stuck her little finger into the lock, and the door opened.

When she was inside she saw the Guardian of the Glass Mountain. 'I am looking for my brothers, the seven ravens,' she said.

'They are not at home,' the Guardian replied. 'But you can wait for them if you like.'

Then he took her into a room where food and drink was laid out for the ravens, on seven little plates and in seven little goblets.

From each plate Anna took a bite to eat, and from each goblet she took a sip to drink, and into the last goblet she dropped the ring her parents had given her. At once she heard a sighing sound in the air and a beating of wings.

The ravens arrived and looked for their food and drink.
Then, one after the other, they said: 'Who has eaten from
my plate? Who has drunk from my goblet?'

As the seventh raven emptied his goblet, out rolled the ring. He looked at it, and he knew it was the ring that belonged to his father and mother. 'If only our sister were here, then the curse would be broken and we would be free,' he said.

When Anna, who was standing behind the door, heard his wish, she stepped forward. At once the ravens were free from the curse and were changed back into her seven brothers.

They were overjoyed to see their sister and to be free at last.

And they all went joyfully home together.